Why the Hyena Does Not Care for Fish

Why the Hyena Does Not Care for Fish

and Other Tales from the Ashanti Gold Weights

PEGGY APPIAH

Illustrated by **Joanna Stubbs**

ANDRE DEUTSCH

First published 1977 by
André Deutsch Limited
105 Great Russell Street London WC1

Copyright © 1977 by Peggy Appiah
Illustrations © 1977 by Joanna Stubbs
All rights reserved

Printed in Great Britain by
Cox & Wyman Ltd
London Fakenham and Reading

ISBN 0 233 96903 9

Contents

An Introduction to
Akan Gold Weights

WEIGHTS WERE USED MANY THOUSANDS OF YEARS BEFORE THE birth of Christ. When towns were first built and people came together to trade, they had to find some way of exchanging goods other than by barter. A man coming to town to sell, for instance, a horse, might not want to exchange it for many baskets of grain! So money was invented, although until someone thought of coins, any small and valuable objects which could be easily carried about were used. But even the use of objects as currency did not really solve the problem because it was necessary to have some sort of standard by which to measure how much you would get for your currency. So weights were invented.

Many different materials were used as weights—glass, pottery, seeds and metal. Metal weights were made in many different shapes and often decorated with designs which made them easier to distinguish. Such weights were known in Egypt and North Africa a thousand years before Christ. They were used by the Phoenicians and the Romans, who carried them far and wide, wherever they went.

Ever since man had begun to travel great distances and to trade in Africa, it had been known that somewhere to the south, beyond the great desert, there were lands rich in gold. Caravans carrying goods such as copper bars, salt, cloth, and beads made the long journey to search for this gold. Sometimes they took one or two years to make the return trip. Sometimes they never returned and were lost, buried in the desert storms. But many did return, laden with gold for the North African and Mediterranean markets.

Great kingdoms grew up and were vanquished. Cities of the African savannah countries were built and destroyed. But trade went on. By the twelfth century AD Mande traders from the Southern Sudan were making regular trips to the forest countries of West Africa from where the gold came. Trading centres such as Begho, in what is now the Brong Ahafo Region of Ghana, grew up where the savannah and forest areas met.

The traders brought their weights with them, some settling in the trading centres. To begin with this gave them an advantage over the gold producers who had nothing to check the weights by. But very soon they made weights locally. As elsewhere early weights were made sometimes of stone, sometimes of pottery and three or four kinds of seeds were used to weigh the small amounts. These seeds continued to be used for as long as there were gold weights.

Early metal weights, from about the thirteenth to fifteenth centuries, were similar to the Mande weights and were related to the Arab weighting system common all over the Sudan and in North Africa. When the Portuguese reached West Africa in the fifteenth century, they found traders already using weights on the Coast.

The main gold-producing areas in what is now Ghana and the Ivory Coast, are occupied by the Akan peoples, all of whom speak similar dialects. They used their weights only to weigh gold, which was sold in the form of gold dust. This was washed from the streams and rivers or mined in shallow mines and pits in the forest. It was even washed from the sand on the sea shore.

With the arrival of the Portuguese and other Europeans the Akan adjusted their weights to the Portuguese and later to the Troy weights which finally became the standard weights of Ghana until the very recent change to the metric system. As trade spread, both to the North and from the Coast, more and more weights were needed. More craftsmen became skilled in their manufacture. Bored with the old designs, craftsmen began to create their own. First they added new designs to the old abstract shapes—swastikas, whorls, bars, pyramids, wavy lines and combs. Then they started to make models of all kinds of familiar objects —swords, birds, hoes, and people; warriors, men carrying weapons and riding horses or working the bellows to keep their metal smelting fires going. By the end of the eighteenth century the skilled craftsmen were making models of most familiar objects which could be represented in weights. They tried everything from elephants to mice, boxes to beetles, sieves to shields, chairs to charms, tortoises to crocodiles and a great variety of human figures doing many different things. The objects the craftsmen could make were almost limitless, but they had to conform to the current weight system.

The Akan were great storytellers, sitting together in the long evenings to exchange tales (it always gets dark about seven in Ghana which is near the equator). In these tales animals took the place of people. In a small village you could say anything about an animal, and if your neighbour recognised himself in your story, he could not blame you, for to do so would be to admit his faults. It is with the weights that tell a story that this book is concerned.

Their language was also rich in proverbs which contained their religious ideas and observations about nature and man such as: 'If I who lie on my back cannot see God, how can you who lie on your stomach?' 'It's a poor man who carries his own tools.' 'You smoke tobacco and carry gunpowder!' There were also weights depicting men with animals or snakes, carrying proverbs like: 'If you take the snake's head, the rest is rope,' or 'You don't jeer at a spitting cobra until you are out of its reach.' Weights were made to illustrate these proverbs and stories or to help people remember the things they did not wish to forget—the designs of individual weapons, the shape of the guns which became familiar after the fifteenth century, the birds and animals they knew so well.

The weights were made by the lost wax process. A model would be made in beeswax and then carefully coated with a mixture of plaster and charcoal and some plant fibres. This would be baked in a charcoal fire until all the wax ran out. Sometimes direct castings were made of seeds of plants, beetles, shrimps or crabs' claws. These would be burnt out like the wax. The hollow mould would then be joined to another crucible containing a lump of brass and both would be heated in the charcoal fire until they were hot enough for the brass to run into the mould. When the mould was cool, it would be broken open and the weight would be removed, and worked on until it was reasonably finished.

Some of the castings were full of detail and difficult to make. Sometimes legs broke off or had to be cut off to make the weight correct; sometimes pieces of metal had to be added to make up weight. Of the million or so weights that were made a good many had small faults, but they could still be used if the weight was correct. The collections which have come down to us today contain a mixture of many dates and qualities. A family weight collection was handed on from generation to generation, new weights being added and old ones being lost or melted down to make new. Any old pieces of brass which were of suitable weight were added. Thus we find old European buckles and buttons, pieces of guns, coins from Holland and France, charms from Devonshire in England, locks, keys, brass fittings off furniture, handles and umbrella tops as well as beads, odd pieces of pottery, antelope's feet, counters for games, teeth, fishbones, stones from inside crocodiles, mixed with the brass weights. Together they tell us much about the Akan peoples, their occupations, and those with whom they traded.

In addition to weights, the *futuo* or packet in which they were bundled contained boxes for gold dust—which was usually tied up in tiny pieces of cloth and fastened with pineapple fibre before being put in the box;— small brushes for brushing up the gold, 'shovels' in which the dust was put so that, when blown gently the dirt could be removed, spoons for picking up the gold dust and scales which were a simple balance with a bar across the top and a pan at each end suspended on three pineapple fibre strings. This was held by a small loop of string tied through a hole in the centre of the bar.

The weights illustrated in this book all come from the forest region of Ghana and were brought to Kumasi, capital of Ashanti, by traders who collected them in the villages. These gold weights were made only by the Akan and were not used after 1900 when their place was taken by modern currency and weights.

11

Why the Hyena
Does Not
Care for Fish

THERE WAS A TIME WHEN THE HYENA AND THE FISH WERE VERY good friends. But, as you know, the hyena is a greedy animal and one day he was so hungry that he decided he would eat fish. He worked out a plan in his head and went to the river.

'Chief Fish!' he called.

The biggest fish put his head out of the river.

'Who calls?' he asked.

'Your friend the hyena.'

'What can I do for you?'

'I have come to challenge your strongest fish to a wrestling match.'

'Hmm,' thought the fish, 'Hmm, he must be plotting some mischief. Whoever heard of a hyena wrestling with a fish!' He sank back into the river to consult his elders, first telling the hyena to come back in the evening.

The hyena ran home to tell his wife he would be bringing her something fine for supper.

The fishes talked and talked but could think of no way out of their trouble. Then the electric fish, who was lying outside the circle, for fear of hurting them, became excited.

'Hey, stop moving about,' said the Chief. 'If you pass any more electricity through the water, the elders will die.'

'I'm sorry,' said the electric fish, 'but I just had an idea. I will lie on the bank and if the hyena tries to trick me, he will see what he will see.'

'A good idea,' said all the fish with relief.

In the evening the hyena came to the river bank and saw the electric fish lying there.

'I don't know you, who are you?' he asked.

'I am the champion wrestler of the fishes' world, no one can come near me.'

'That we shall see,' said the hyena who had never heard of an electric fish, and he leapt on the fish. 'I am going to eat you,' he cried.

Those were his last words to the fish. For the electric fish gave him

13

one flip with his tail that gave him such a shock he fell back unconscious.

The fish slipped back into the river.

That evening the hyena dragged himself home, his legs wobbled, his head throbbed and he swore to himself that he would never, never go after fish again.

How the Deer
Lost its Long Horns

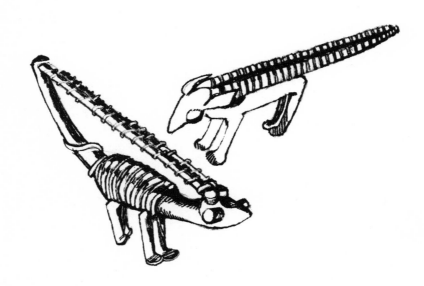

16

ONCE THE DEER HAD SUCH LONG AND STRONG HORNS THAT IT was feared by all the other animals. It was always wounding them accidentally. So they got together to discuss how to protect themselves.

The deer was as anxious as they were to be at peace. Together they decided that the best thing would be to push the horns down a little.

The animals pushed and pushed and pushed.

They pushed so hard that the horns nearly disappeared.

When the deer realised how necessary the horns had been for his defence, it was, alas, too late. From that time to this he has been forced to rely on his swiftness to escape from trouble.

Thus the elders say: 'Had I known is always too late.' '*Nim-saa ka akyire.*'

The Leopard's Drum

LEOPARD HAD A BIG DRUM. IT WAS AN ENORMOUS DRUM, THE biggest drum in the world.

The Sky God envied him the drum and wanted to get it. The elephant offered, the lion offered, the deer offered and even the crocodile said he could get the drum. But they could not.

Then the little tortoise said, 'I will get you the drum.' How the animals laughed at him. But he did not mind. 'Wait,' he said, 'you will see.'

Tortoise went slowly to Leopard's house and looked around.

'What do you want?' asked Leopard.

'Oh, I just wanted to see your drum. The Sky God has made an enormous one and I wanted to make sure it is really bigger than yours.'

Leopard showed him the drum.

'Yes,' he said, 'the Sky God's is bigger.'

'There is no drum bigger than mine!' Leopard was annoyed.

'His is big enough to get inside. I am sure you can't get into yours.'

'Oh yes I can!' Leopard started to crawl into the hollow bottom of his drum. His tail stayed outside and swung angrily back and forth.

'Your tail is right outside,' said Tortoise. 'You must go farther, still farther; that's right you're nearly there.' With a final struggle Leopard disappeared inside his drum.

Tortoise quickly blocked the end with some strong pieces of wood he was carrying.

'Let me out!' growled Leopard. 'Stop playing with me.'

But Tortoise wasn't playing.

Leopard started to roar, but he was fixed tightly in the drum and it was a strong drum indeed.

Tortoise tied the drum to his back and ambled slowly, oh, so slowly, towards the Sky God's home. It took a long, long time to get there.

At long last Tortoise came in front of the Sky God.

'I have brought the drum,' he said, 'and Leopard is inside it. What do you want to do with him?'

The other animals gathered round in wonder. 'Kill him,' they said.

'Don't kill me!' pleaded Leopard. 'You can have the drum. Only let me go.'

The Sky God laughed. 'I think he has been punished enough,' he said. 'Let him out!' So Tortoise let out the leopard.

The Sky God asked Tortoise what he would like as a reward.

Tortoise, knowing the jealousy of the other animals and the anger of the leopard, said, a little thoughtfully, 'I would like a hard cover. One that would protect me from violence.'

That is why Tortoise has a hard shell. Before that his skin was as soft as that of a lizard.

The Spotted Cow

THERE WAS ONCE A RICH CHIEF WHO WISHED TO FIND OUT WHO was the cleverest of his subjects.

At the time of the yam festival he took his biggest and fattest cow and offered it as a prize to anyone who could spend the night in a small room he had built, without scratching themselves. The room was full of mosquitoes.

One after another the villagers tried but failed. How those mosquitoes bit. It was impossible not to scratch.

At last Kwaku Ananse offered to try. He went into the room and closed the door. A lamp burnt on a shelf so that the Chief's attendant, watching through a hole in the wooden walls, could see every action.

As soon as Kwaku entered the room the mosquitoes attacked him. He wandered over to the wall where he knew the attendant stood.

'Is it true that the cow has a white face?' he asked, wiping his hands all over his face.

'It's true,' said the man.

'Is it true that it has spots, here and here and here?' Kwaku slapped himself all over.

'Quite true,' said the man.

'Has it very fat legs like this?' Kwaku lifted up one leg after another, pinching and patting them.

'That's the one,' said the man.

And so it went on.

Kwaku stayed all night. In the morning when he came out the attendant swore he had not scratched himself—he had only talked to him about the cow.

So Kwaku Ananse won the cow and the Chief knew who was the wisest man in town.

23

Why the Crow
Is Partly Black

WHEN GOD THE CREATOR HAD FINISHED MAKING THE WORLD, he made the birds. He told them he wanted the wisest among them to become his priest. Finally he chose the crow.

God made the crow pure white and sent it into the world to see what was happening there. He told him to come soon with the news.

The crow went into the world and flew here and there, looking and listening. On his way to look for man he came to a ground-nut farm.

'It won't hurt to rest a little and eat a little,' he thought.

He landed on the farm and started to eat.

My, those nuts were good. He forgot all about time and ate and ate and ate.

Time passed. When Crow had eaten, he slept. Then he was hungry again and he ate.

God waited impatiently for his messenger. At last, fearing something had happened to him, he sent the bul-bul to find out where he was.

The bul-bul saw the crow and flew straight back to God to tell where he was.

When the crow finally returned, God was very, very angry with him. He refused to make him his priest. As a sign of his anger he took all the white from the crow except for his collar.

The crow perched miserably on a tree and cried in its sorrow:

> Saa, saa, saa . . .
> Has it come to that, has it come to that.

The old people say that it is because he failed to fulfil his errand that he laments aloud. A permanent warning to the disobedient.

Why the Snake
Caught the Hornbill

THE HORNBILL WAS GREEDY AND ALWAYS IN DEBT.

One day he went to the snake for money.

'Lend me some money, I beg you,' he said. 'I will pay it back with interest.'

'When will you pay me?' asked the snake.

'Soon, very soon.'

So the snake lent the hornbill some money.

Weeks passed and he did not repay it. The snake saw him one day on the branch of a tree and called up to him:

'Where is my money. You promised to repay me.'

'Ha, ha, ha,' cried the hornbill, 'you can't catch me.' And he flew off.

'Wait and see,' hissed the snake.

Months passed. The rains ceased and one by one the streams and pools in the forest dried up. At last there was only the one drinking pool left.

The snake went to the pool and waited.

In the evening the hornbill flew down to drink with the other birds and animals.

The snake slid from the undergrowth and 'snap' he had the hornbill.

'Let me go,' shrieked the hornbill. 'You shall have your money.'

'Why should I?' said the snake. 'I, too, am hungry.' So he ate the hornbill.

Thus the old people say: 'The horned snake lying on the ground has caught the hornbill from the sky.'

Why the Hunter
Lost his Head

THERE WAS ONCE A HUNTER WHO WENT EVERY DAY TO THE forest to hunt for game. One day, as he went, he heard sweet music. He went slowly towards it and there, in a small clearing, he saw a tortoise playing on a small stringed instrument and singing to his heart's content.

The hunter walked across the clearing and looked at the tortoise.

'I could take you and eat you,' he said, 'but instead I will take you to play to the Chief. He will reward me.'

'You'd better not,' said the tortoise. 'I prefer it here in the forest. You are asking for trouble. I warn you to leave me alone.'

The hunter laughed, picked up the tortoise and took him to the village. He went straight to the Chief and told him of the wonder. The Chief did not believe him.

'If what you say is true, then you shall have a big reward; if not, then you will lose your head.' He called all the people together to listen to the tortoise.

Soon there was a big crowd. The hunter took the tortoise from his bag and put him and his instrument on the ground, in front of the Chief.

'Play!' he said. 'Play for the Chief.'

The tortoise just blinked its eyes and looked stupid.

'Hurry up,' warned the Chief, 'or you will lose your head.'

The hunter went on his knees to the tortoise, reminded him how he had saved his life. 'Play!' he begged. 'Play just one little tune.'

The tortoise just looked stupid.

The Chief grew angry. 'Oh, Hunter!' he said. 'I warned you I would stand no trickery. If the tortoise does not sing at once, you will lose your head.'

The tortoise refused to sing and the hunter was led off by the executioner.

'Swish, swish,' went the sword. The hunter's head rolled on the ground.

The crowd sighed and turned to go. But the moment the hunter's

29

head rolled on the ground, a change came over the tortoise.

He picked up his instrument and in a thin piping voice he sang:

> Trouble does not look for man,
> It is man who looks for trouble.

The people were amazed.

The Chief was amazed.

They were afraid of the little tortoise and the Chief ordered that he be taken back to the forest and left alone. From that day to this the people in his village never touch the tortoise.

It is said that sometimes on a moonlight night they hear singing from the forest. If they listen carefully they hear the words:

> Trouble does not look for man,
> It is man who looks for trouble.

The Bread-Winner

ABENA WAS THE ONLY DAUGHTER OF A POOR WIDOW. SHE WAS very beautiful and when she was old enough to marry, her mother asked the Queen Mother to find her a good husband.

The Queen Mother consulted the Chief and together they decided that all the girl's suitors should compete for her hand. Which ever could tell the longest tale should marry Abena.

The day of the competition arrived and the first suitor started his story. He was a herdsman, used to being out with his flocks all day and was short of words, so he soon came to a standstill. The next was a trader, but he did little better. Many tried but few succeeded in talking for very long.

At last a handsome young farmer stepped out of the crowd. He bowed to the Chief and the Queen Mother, then he told the following tale:

'There was once a bird which laid some eggs in a nest on the branch of a tree. The eggs soon hatched out and the bird flew off to find food for her young. She fed them; they grew hungry again and she flew off to find food. She fed them; they grew hungry again and she flew off to find food. She fed them; they grew hungry . . .'

And so he went on and on until the people put their hands over their ears and said, 'Stop, stop.'

'But there is no end to my story,' replied the young man.

'Then you have won,' said the Chief. 'Go and take the girl and look after her well.'

The young man went up to Abena and took her hand.

'When we are married,' he said, 'you will have children. When you and they are hungry, I will work to get food for you, but you will hunger again. There is no end to the story. That is life.'

So they were married, and because the young man worked hard and was clever, they lived happily ever after.

How the Hoe
Came to Ashanti

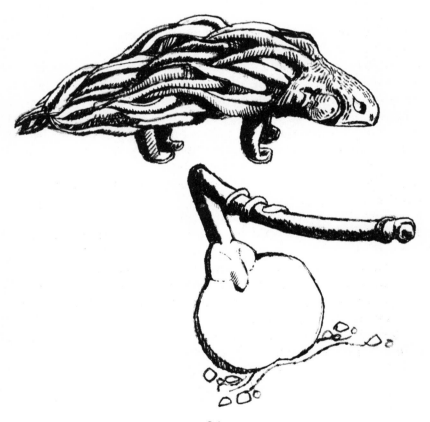

ONCE THERE WAS ONLY ONE HOE, IT BELONGED TO KOTOKO THE porcupine and he used it on his farm in Ashanti. One year Ananse the Spider asked if he could share a new farm that Porcupine was making. Porcupine agreed. Every day they would go out to the farm. When Ananse and his family had finished weeding and went home to lunch, Porcupine would arrive. He would take up his hoe and say:

Gyensaworowa, Kotoko saworowa,
Gyensaworowa, Kotoko saworowa,
Gyensaworowa.

and the hoe would start working. Porcupine sat with his chewing-stick under the tree while the hoe worked and worked and cleared the land. In the evening he took it home and hid it in his house.

Now Kwaku Ananse wondered how he could clear so much land in one day so he hid behind a tree and watched the wonderful hoe at work. He was determined to steal it.

One night he crept into Kotoko's house and stole the hoe. Very early in the morning he went to the farm with the hoe and used the magic words:

Gyensaworowa, Kotoko saworowa,

and the hoe started working. It went on and on. At last when Kwaku Ananse thought it had done enough he told it to stop. Alas, he had not learnt the magic words to stop it and the hoe would not. Instead it went on and on, and on and on, across forest and desert, sea and mountain, until it came to England.

The English people liked it so much that they made copies, but they too could not stop it, and so it went on and over the edge of the world.

By and by the English people exported the hoes to Ashanti where they are used till this day.

Once there was only one hoe and that belonged to the porcupine in Ashanti.

35

Abena and the Bush-Cow

THERE WAS ONCE A GIRL CALLED ABENA. WHEN SHE GREW UP she was very beautiful, but she refused to marry anyone her parents chose.

'When I find the man I want,' she said, 'then I will come and take my father's snuff box and hit him on the head with it.'

Time passed. Many young men came to the house but Abena refused them all.

There lived in the near-by forest a herd of bush-cows. One of them heard of the beauty of Abena and turned himself into a man. He was as handsome as a fairy-tale prince. When Abena saw him, she ran to where her father was playing draughts with his friends; she took her father's snuff box and hit him hard on the head.

'At last,' said her father. 'At last,' said the elders. 'At last,' said all the villagers.

So they were married and Abena was given many gifts. The couple stayed for three days in the village, making merry. Then the man said to his wife: 'I must go to my own village.' 'I will come with you,' she said. 'We must send her with a fitting escort,' said the people.

So Abena was given twenty-four people to carry her things to her husband's village. Early in the morning they set off through the forest. It was cool and sweet under the trees and as they went they sang.

They came to a clearing in the forest and the man turned to his wife. 'Now I must tell you the truth, Abena, I must tell you who I really am. Look, I make *pa* I make *gyiren*'—and he turned into a bush-cow.

'What has happened?' cried the people. 'What did he say?'

'He just said "I make *pa*, I make *gyiren*,"' replied Abena, and she too turned into a bush-cow.

'Eh!' said all the people. 'She said "I make *pa*, I make *gyiren*"' and they too turned into bush-cows; all except one, who ran back to the village.

He called the people together and told them the tale. As soon as he said 'I make *pa*, I make *gyiren*,' he too became a bush-cow. And so it went

on until all the villagers turned into bush-cows and ran off into the forest. One old woman remained alone.

One day a medicine man came to the village. He looked around but no one was there. Then he shouted out, '*Dinn, dinn, dinn.*' There was only an echo and the buzz of insects. 'That's funny,' he thought, 'a big village but no people.'

As he went, he met the old woman.

'You are a witch,' he said. 'You have eaten up all the people. I must kill you at once.'

'Don't do that!' begged the old woman. 'Rather bind me to a tree and I will tell you what has happened.' The medicine man took strong creepers and bound her to a tree. She started the tale, but when she said, 'I make *pa*, I make *gyiren*,' the creepers burst and the old woman buffalo blundered off into the forest.

The medicine man and his followers took a big brass pan. Into it they put all manner of herbs, mixing them with water. They carried it into the forest until they came to the glade. There they saw a huge herd of bush-cows. The man took his cow-tail switch and dipped it in the basin. He sprinkled all the animals with the water.

Lo and behold, the villagers stood there. The real buffaloes ran off into the forest.

That is how life came back to the village and also it is why the Ekuona clan chose the bush-cow as their emblem.

The Elephant
and the Sunbird

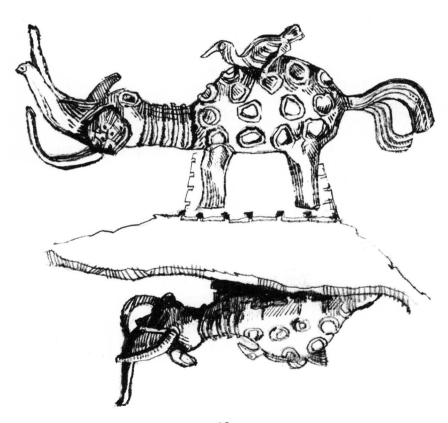

ONE DAY KWAKU ANANSE VISITED THE SKY GOD. THE SKY GOD
was sucking half a lime. When Kwaku left he handed him the second
half.

'What can I do with it?' thought Kwaku. 'I don't like lime.'

As he went he saw a woman washing clothes in the river. The child
on her back was crying, so he gave it the lime. The woman gave him a
calabash full of water.

He went a little farther. He saw a man digging yams and sweating
heavily. He gave him the water to drink. The man gave him a yam.

He went a little farther and saw a blacksmith chewing charcoal. He
gave him the yam to eat instead. The blacksmith gave him a cutting tool.

He went a little farther, and met a farmer. The farmer was cutting
palm-nuts with his leg. He gave him the cutting tool and the farmer
gave him a pot of palm oil.

He went a little farther and met a woman trying to oil her child with
spital. He gave her the pot of oil. The woman gave him one of her
children.

He went a little farther and met a sad young woman wandering in the
forest. On her back she had tied a wooden spoon and put beads round
it, as if it was indeed a child. He gave her the child and she in joy gave
him the spoon, which had a grinder on one end.

He went a little farther and came to a hut in the forest. In front of it
sat a woman, trying to grind corn with her elbow. He gave her the spoon
and she gave him a jar of corn wine.

He went a little farther and met some elephants drinking muddy
water from a dried-up pond. He gave one the corn wine.

'I have nothing to give you,' said the elephant, 'but if anyone falls
into the ditch when we jump it, you can take him home.'

The elephants all jumped the ditch, but the last one was careless. He
stumbled and fell. Kwaku helped it get up and tied a rope round its leg
and told it to come home with him.

So he started for home with the elephant.

41

As he went, he saw a beautiful little sunbird, drinking the nectar from a flowering bush. He stopped to look.

'How my children would love the bird,' he said. He ran after it through the bush, dropping the rope on the path. The bird flitted from tree to tree, always out of reach. At last it flew away, right through the trees and over the river.

Kwaku turned back and remembered his elephant. Of course, when he reached the path the elephant had wandered off and gone back to the herd.

Thus the old people say: 'Don't leave an elephant and chase after a sunbird.' Don't lose something big and important because of a little thing.

The Hunter and the Leopard

THERE WAS FAMINE IN THE LAND AND EVERYONE WENT HUNGRY.
Even the great hunter Asemieri could find no food.

One day as he was going home Asemieri heard a loud cry from a
near-by tree. He forced himself through the dry undergrowth and looking up he saw a large leopard caught firmly in the forked branch of a
tree.

'However did you get up there?' he asked, curiously.

'Please help me down!' cried the leopard. 'I met Elephant on the path
and he was so hungry and angry he lost his temper. He just threw me
up here and here I am stuck.'

Now Asemieri was fearless, so he climbed the tree and after much
struggling, released the leopard. He expected it to be grateful. Instead
the leopard demanded food.

The hunter was so sorry for him that he gave him one of his hunting
dogs to eat. Alas, this was not enough. He seized the second one and
when he had gulped it down he said to the hunter:

'I am still hungry. Give me something else.'

The hunter shook his head. 'I have given you all I have, and you have
taken my dogs which helped me to work, how can I give you anything
else?'

'Then I shall eat you,' said the leopard, who was standing between
the hunter and his gun.

As they were talking Tortoise came along and demanded to hear the
story. 'I will decide,' he said firmly, 'if the leopard should eat Asemieri.
But first I simply don't believe that Leopard could have been up in the
tree at all. Show me what happened and I will judge between you.'

Leopard leapt into the tree to show Tortoise just how he had been
stuck—and he got stuck again.

Tortoise turned to Asemieri. 'Quick, get your gun, shoot him at
once, the ungrateful creature, and don't be so soft again.'

He waddled off into the undergrowth and Asemieri fetched his gun.
He took careful aim and shot the leopard.

45

Why the Leopard Has Spots

ALL THE ANIMALS WERE GOING TO A FUNERAL. AS THEY WENT
they passed by a garden-egg farm, full of wonderful, ripe garden-eggs.

Now the leopard had a passion for garden-eggs. He slipped from the
path and started to eat. He ate and he ate until half of the crop was
consumed. Then he rejoined the path and went on his way.

Soon after the farmer reached his farm. When he saw what had
happened he ran after the animals, cursing and swearing and accusing
them of stealing his crop. This all the animals denied warmly.

'Will you prove it?' asked the farmer.

'How?' asked the animals.

'I will build a fire and you will all jump over it. He who falls in the
fire will be the thief.'

The animals agreed and the leopard smiled to himself. It was not
possible that he, the great leopard, could fall in the fire.

One by one the animals jumped. Even the little mouse managed
somehow. When it came to the leopard's turn, he ran to the fire, he got
ready to spring, he leapt into the air—but he forgot the garden-eggs
which lay heavy in his stomach. Instead of coming down on the other
side of the fire he fell short and rolled in the embers. He howled and
rushed from the fire, but not soon enough.

The fire had burnt patches on his fur, some brown, some black. The
animals stared in amazement and then started to hoot at him and cry
out, 'Thief, thief.'

He turned tail and ran. And so from that day to this the leopard
carries a spotted coat in memory of his greed.

The Stolen Sheep

A MAN ONCE STOLE A SHEEP. HE WAS AFRAID OF BEING CAUGHT, so he gave it to his son to sell.

The boy tied the sheep under a tree near the market and because it was early, went to play with his friends.

By-and-by he came back. The sheep was nowhere to be seen. He searched and searched but he could ask no questions as the sheep had been stolen.

Late in the evening he returned slowly home, thinking and thinking what he could tell his father. His pockets were empty. At last he had an idea.

His father was waiting anxiously for him. 'Why have you been so long?' he asked. 'How much did you get for the sheep?'

'Well, father, I bargained hard and long but I am afraid that I only managed to get what you gave for it.'

Do you think he was clever enough to avoid punishment?

Failure of a Pact

ONCE THE ANIMALS AND THE BIRDS MADE AN AGREEMENT TO help protect each other from man, the predator.

The birds in the sky could see much farther than the animals on the ground and they were to warn them of man's approach. If any bird was in trouble near the ground, the animals would go to its aid.

For a bit the plan worked. Men wondered why the animals always disappeared when they came near. Then they heard the calls of the birds and came to distinguish the warning notes. These also told them where the animals were.

One day a bush-cow was caught in a trap. The little Opaaben fluttered round and did all it could to release the great animal. Alas, the trap was too heavy and the bird too small. He could only call out to the bush-cow:

Perete, perete, perete.
Struggle, struggle, struggle.

'Or,' it said, 'the hunter who lives in Akua Konadu's house will come and get you and your head will taste good in the soup.'

Buee, buee, bueee.
Very, very good.
Perete, perete, perete.

Alas, the warnings of the bird were in vain, for the bush-cow could not struggle enough. Akua Konadu says that its head did indeed taste delicious in the soup.

How the Butterfly Cheated the Grasshopper

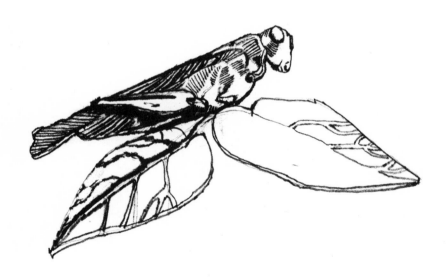

ONCE UPON A TIME THE GRASSHOPPER AND THE BUTTERFLY
went to work on a farm together.

At the end of the day they were paid threepence for their work. The
butterfly took the money and gave the grasshopper one penny as his
share.

The grasshopper went home, singing to himself.

'How much did you get?' asked his wife. 'We were paid threepence
and here is my share.' He handed his wife a penny. 'But this is not
half, the butterfly has cheated you. Go back and get the rest.'

But the butterfly just laughed and flew away. The grasshopper chased
after, hopping from plant to plant. As he went he cried:

> *Pe—pe—pe, wankye no pe, pe, pe, pe.*
> *Kwabena Kuma wankye no pe.*
> *Ye nyinaa yerekye no pe, pe, pe, pe.*
> Equally, equally, equally, you did
>   not share it equally.
> Kwabena Kuma, you did not share it
>   equally,
> We are all going to divide it equally,
>   equally, equally.

And that is what you hear him singing to this day.

Why the Snake
Takes Poison
from the Frog

IN SOME PARTS OF GHANA IT IS BELIEVED THAT THE FROG GIVES the snake poison. People say that the snake squeezes the frog and turns it over and over to get out all the poison.

Once upon a time the frog and the snake had an argument as to which was the most poisonous. In the end they decided to have a test to find out. Each in turn would bite a man while the other appeared in front of him. Which ever bite proved the most dangerous would be proved the most poisonous.

First snake bit a man and the frog appeared to him. The man went home and though he was ill he recovered quickly.

Then the frog bit a man and the snake appeared.

He rushed home crying out, 'It has killed me, it has killed me.' Very soon he died.

The snake had to admit that the frog's bite was the more poisonous and ever since he has gone to the frog for his poison.

But I think the man died of fright, don't you?

How the Parrot
Scared
the Highwayman